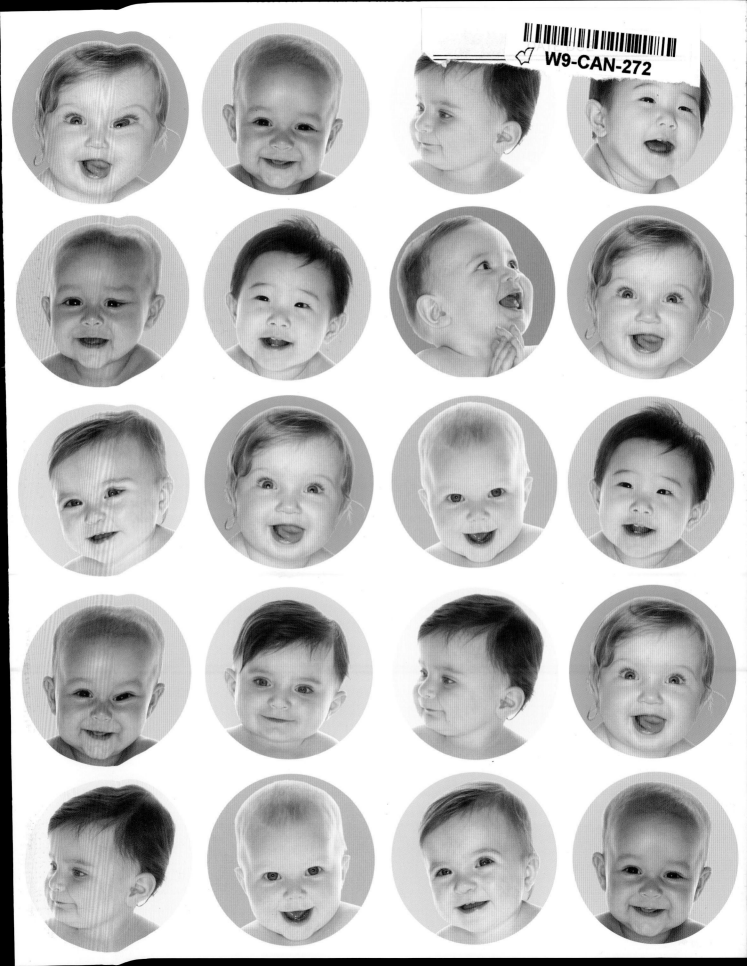

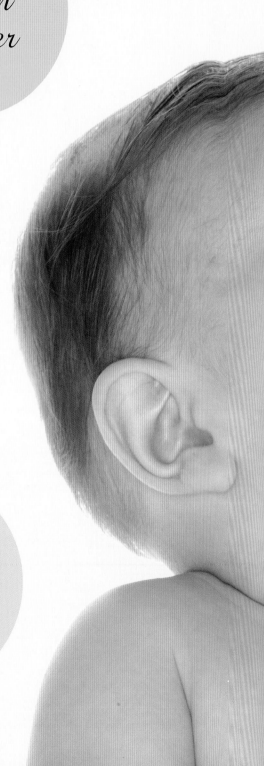

concept and words by
Lynn Reiser

photographs by
Penny Gentieu

Alfred A. Knopf
New York

You
and
Me,
Baby

Hey, baby!

Look at you, looking at me,

looking at you, looking at me.

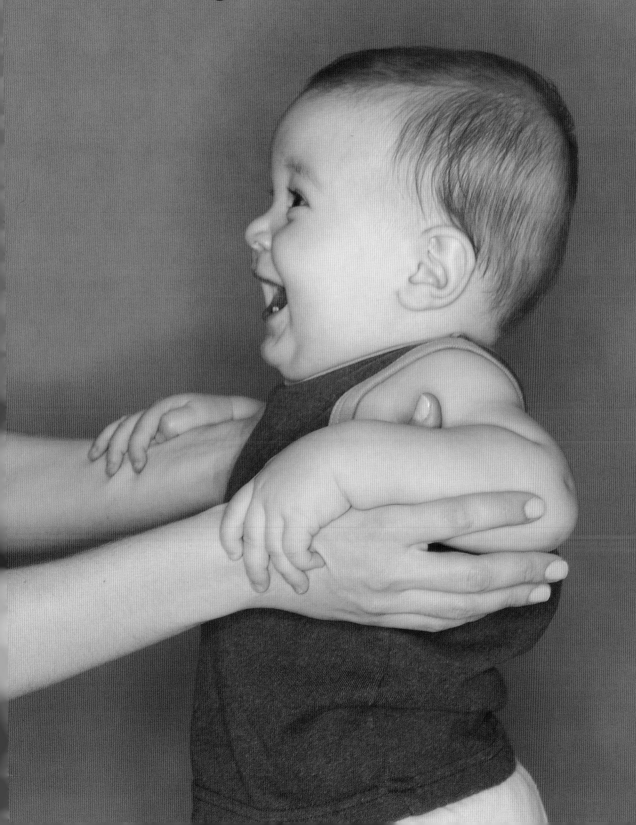

Wow, baby!

Look at you,
waving at me,

waving at you,

waving at me.

Now, baby!
Look at me,
smiling at you,

smiling at me,

feeding you,

feeding me,

feeding you!

Mmmm, baby,
hug me,
hugging you,
hugging me,

hugging you!

Ooooh, baby!

Look at you,
splashing me,
splashing you.

Peek at me, peeking at you, peeking at me.
PEEK-A-

BOO!

Oh, baby!

Look at you,
looking at me,

laughing at me,
laughing at you!

It's you and me,

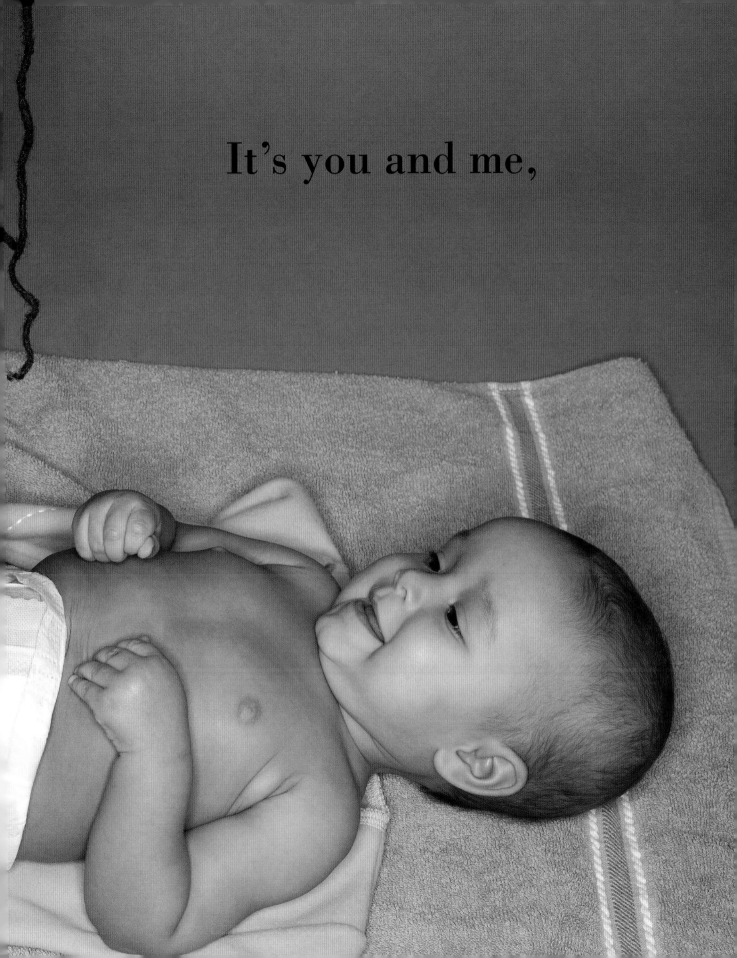

and me
and you,

just you and me,
baby!

A valentine for Morton
— L. R.

To Audrey and Anna, my loving mother and sweet daughter
— P. G.

THIS IS A BORZOI BOOK PUBLISHED BY ALFRED A. KNOPF

Text copyright © 2006 by Lynn Reiser
Photographs copyright © 2006 by Penny Gentieu

Published in the United States by Alfred A. Knopf, an imprint of Random House
Children's Books, a division of Random House, Inc., New York.

KNOPF, BORZOI BOOKS, and the colophon are registered trademarks of Random House, Inc.

www.randomhouse.com/kids

Educators and librarians, for a variety of teaching tools, visit us at
www.randomhouse.com/teachers

Library of Congress Cataloging-in-Publication Data
Reiser, Lynn.
You and me, baby / Lynn Reiser ; [illustrations by Penny Gentieu]. —1st ed.
p.   cm.
SUMMARY: Photographs and simple text portray interactions between babies and parents.
ISBN: 0-375-83401-X (trade) — ISBN: 0-375-93401-4 (lib. bdg.)
ISBN-13: 978-0-375-83401-1 (trade) — ISBN-13: 978-0-375-93401-8 (lib. bdg.)
[1. Parent and child—Fiction. 2. Babies—Fiction. 3. Stories in rhyme.]
I. Gentieu, Penny, ill. II. Title.
PZ8.3.R2757You 2006
[E]—dc22
2005021581

MANUFACTURED IN CHINA

10 9 8 7 6 5 4 3 2
First Edition